The clothes we wear

This edition first published in 2006
by The Evans Publishing Group
2A Portman Mansions
Chiltern Street
London
W1U 6NR

Reprinted 2010

British Library Cataloguing in Publication data.
A catalogue record for this book is available from the British Library.

Printed in Hong Kong by New Era Printing Co. Ltd.

ISBN 978 0 237 53131 7

ACKNOWLEDGEMENTS:
Editorial: Louise John
Design: D.R.ink
Production: Jenny Mulvanny

PHOTOGRAPHS: Micheal Stannard, except for the following:

Pages 8-9: silkworm (Bruce Coleman Ltd), flax plant (Robert Harding Picture Library), cotton plant
(The Image Bank), acrylic fibre manufacture (The Image Bank); page 11: Tuareg man in robes (Robert
Harding); page 13: sheep (Bruce Coleman Ltd); page 14: cyclist (The Image Bank), baseball player
(Robert Harding), ice-hockey player (The Image Bank), fencer (Robert Harding), modern swimmer
(Robert Harding), early 20th-century swimmer (Robert Harding); pages 16-17: builder (Robert Harding),
surgeon (The Image Bank), surgeon's gloves (Robert Harding); pages 18-19: fishermen (The Image
Bank), fireman (The Image Bank), astronaut (The Image Bank); page 23: clogs (Robert Harding); pages
26-27: Western woman in sarong (The Image Bank), Indonesian women in sarongs (Robert Harding),
Native American moccasins (Robert Harding); page 28: (top right) Chateau Watches Ltd, (bottom left)
Sue Potts, (bottom right) Victoria and Albert Museum; page 29: Sue Potts.
Based on the original edition of The Clothes We Wear published in 1997

The authors and publishers would like to thank the following companies for their kind help with the
objects photographed for this book:
A special thank you to John Lewis department store, Bristol and to these Bristol stores and shops:
Debenhams, Mothercare, Shoe Express, Mastershoe, Saxone, Oxfam, Dancewell, Whose Sport, Tumi
of Bath (Bristol branch) and Oswald Bailey.

Many thanks also to:
Sue Wollatt/Graham-Cameron Illustration Agency, for border artworks on cover and inside, and eye-
opener logo; Julia and Jane of Little Women, Hebron House, Bristol, for making the waistcoats on
pages 20-21 and supplying fabrics and advice; Claudia Pagliaraui for the artworks on pages 20-21;
Next Retail; and, most importantly, to our models: Jordan Smith (pages 6, 7, 12, 21), Rosie Crews
(pages 6, 7, 10), Michelle Man (cover and pages 7, 13,) Marie Attwood (pages 10, 21) and Julia Pearce
(page 19).

The clothes we wear

Sally Hewitt and Jane Rowe

Evans

About this book

The LOOK AROUND YOU books have been put together in a way that makes them ideal for teachers and parents to share with young children. Take time over each question and project. Have fun learning about how all sorts of different homes, clothes, toys and everyday objects have been designed for a special purpose.

THE CLOTHES WE WEAR deals with the kinds of ideas about design and technology that many children will be introduced to in their early years at school. The pictures and text will encourage children to explore design on the page, and all around them. This book will help them to understand some of the basic rules about why items of clothing are made from particular materials and are a certain shape, and why they are suited to certain occasions and are easy to wear. It will also help them to develop their own design skills.

The 'eye opener' boxes reveal interesting and unusual facts, or lead children to examine one aspect of design. There are also activities that put theory into practice in an entertaining and informative way. Children learn most effectively by joining in, talking, asking questions and solving problems, so encourage them to talk about what they are doing and to find ways of solving the problems for themselves.

Try to make thinking about design and technology a part of everyday life. Just pick up any object around the house and talk about why it has been made that way, and how it could be improved. Design is not just a subject for adults. You can have a lot of fun with it at any age - and develop artistic flair and practical skills.

Contents

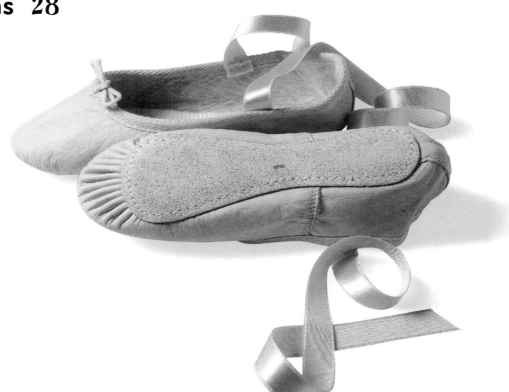

The clothes we wear

Every morning, you choose what **clothes** you are going to wear for the day.

Look at the clothes Ellie and Sam are **wearing**.

Where do you think they are **going?**

What do you think they will be **doing?**

What clothes did you put on this **morning?**

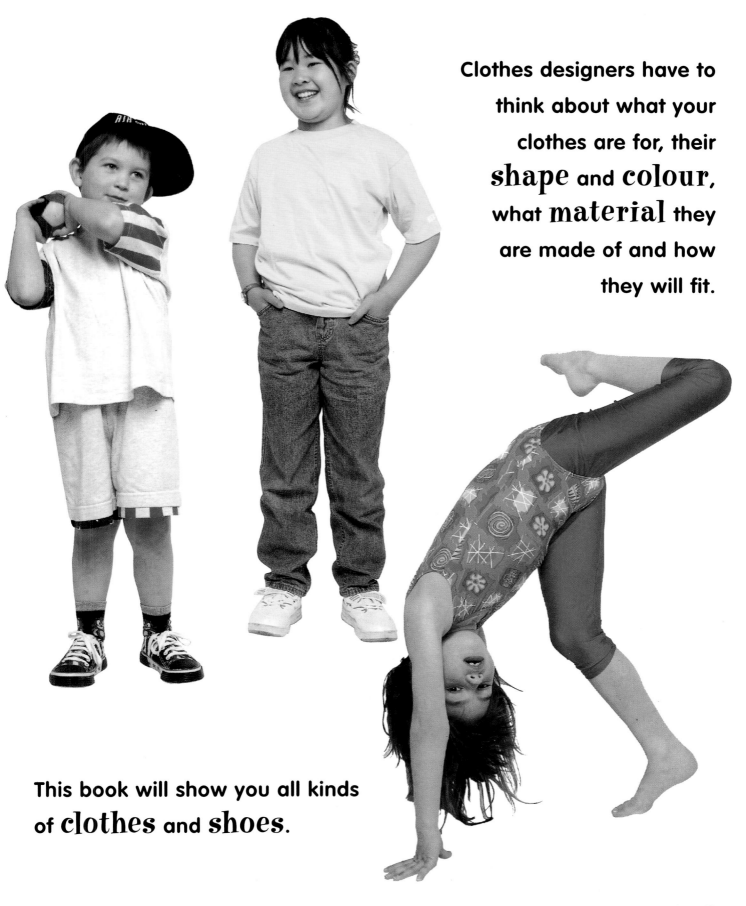

Clothes designers have to think about what your clothes are for, their **shape** and **colour**, what **material** they are made of and how they will fit.

This book will show you all kinds of **clothes** and **shoes**.

Different materials

Do the **clothes** you are wearing feel soft, rough or silky?

Materials can come from animals, plants or be man made.

Wool mostly comes from sheep. It is soft and warm.

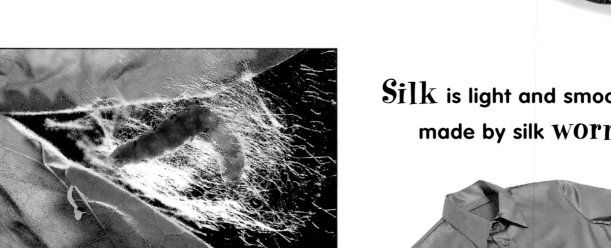

Silk is light and smooth. It is made by silk **worms**.

Cotton and linen come from plants. Linen is from the flax plant and is very **strong**.

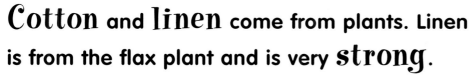

Polyester and nylon come from oil.

Chemicals from oil make a special kind of plastic, which is squeezed through tiny holes to make threads.

9

Keeping cool

These clothes have been designed to keep you **cool** in hot weather.

A **hat** can protect your head from the sun.

Cotton clothes help to keep you cool.

Sandals let air in and stop your feet getting hot.

Leave a white and a black T-shirt in the **sun** for ten minutes and then feel them. Which one feels **hotter?**

Which one would you **rather** wear on a hot day?

People in hot countries often wear long, loose robes to protect them from the sun.

Air moves around inside the robes and helps to keep them cool.

Keeping warm and dry

These clothes will help to keep you **warm** and **dry** in cold and wet weather.

A lot of **body heat** escapes through your head. A warm **hat** can help to keep your whole body warm.

This padded **coat** keeps you warm – just like a duvet!

Sheep keep dry because their coats are oily. The raindrops roll off their wool.

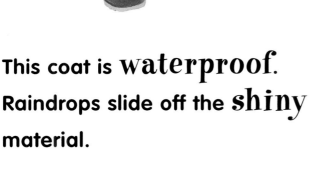

This coat is made of material that has been rubbed with oil to make it waterproof.

This coat is **waterproof**. Raindrops slide off the **shiny** material.

What **else** can you see on this page that is waterproof?

Sportswear

There are specially designed clothes and shoes for every different sport.

Cyclists wear helmets to protect their heads in case they have an accident.

Fluorescent clothes glow in the dark so that the cyclist can be spotted.

Gloves have leather palms for gripping the handlebars firmly.

In sports like ice hockey, baseball and fencing, players wear special pads, helmets and masks to **protect** themselves.

Many years ago, women covered up well when they went swimming.
Modern swimsuits are designed for speeding through the water.

Clothes for protection

Some clothes and shoes have been specially designed to protect people while they work.

A building site worker should always wear a **hard hat**.

Builder's boots have tough soles and **steel-capped** toes.

Surgeons have to keep clean to protect
their patients from germs.

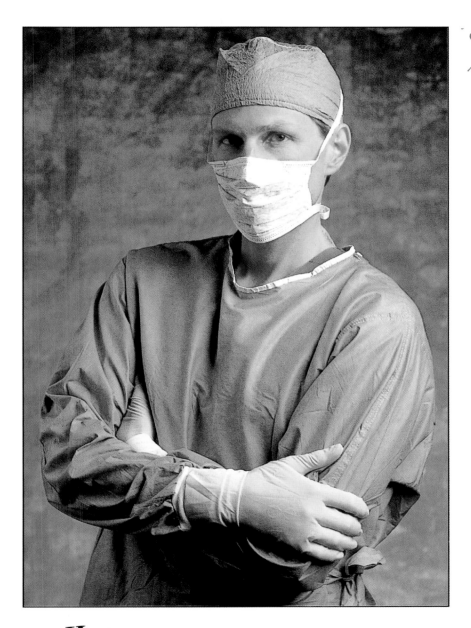

Surgeons use
their hands for
very delicate
work, so their
gloves have to fit
like a second skin.

Hats completely cover their hair.
They wear a mask over their
nose and mouth.

Clothes to work in

You can often guess what sort of work someone does because of the clothes they wear.

Fishermen wear waterproof clothes to keep them dry in stormy seas.

Fire fighters wear special clothing to protect them from smoke and fire.

A track suit allows a sports teacher to **move** around easily and keeps her **warm** when she is standing still.

Humans cannot survive in space, so a space suit is designed for an astronaut to live in. An oxygen tank gives the astronaut air to breathe.

Make a waistcoat

1. First, get someone to measure your chest size with a tape measure. Add a few centimetres to allow for the seams of the waistcoat.

2. Now divide this figure into 2. This is how big the back of your waistcoat should be. The front is the same size, only it is cut into 2 pieces.

3. Cut out your material in pieces like the ones shown below. You could try first with paper and then pin your paper pieces to your material and cut around them. Get a grown-up to help you with the pins and cutting.

4. Now sew the pieces together. Backstitch is a good stitch to use.

5. Do you want ribbon ties or buttons? If you want buttons, make button holes by cutting slits and then sewing over the edges with blanket stitch to stop them fraying.

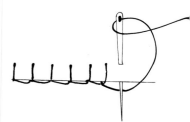

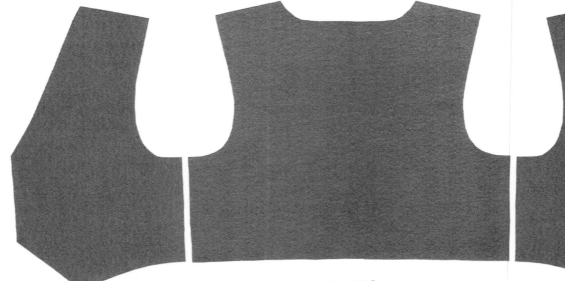

LEFT FRONT   BACK   RIGHT FRONT

Can you see where **blanket stitch** has been used?

What other ways can you think of to **decorate** your waistcoat?

Shoes

Shoes protect your **feet** and should be comfortable to wear.

Leather is good for making shoes because it is tough but bends easily. It also lets **air** through to your feet.

Which of these shoes would be the **fastest** to put on?

Which of these shoes would be the best for running around in?

These boots are **warm** and waterproof and good for the **winter**.

Flip flops are great to wear when you are playing on the **beach**. They are **cool** in warm weather.

eye opener

Clogs are carved from wood to fit the shape of your feet. Do you think they are comfortable to wear?

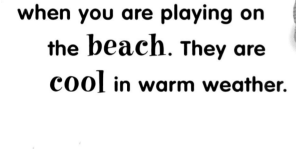

Soles

The sole is the part of your shoe that leaves a **footprint**.

↑ The soles of these walking boots can **grip** rough ground.

◄ Thick soles filled with **air** make the ground feel softer.

➡ Football boots have screw-in **studs** to stop you slipping on wet grass and mud.

◀ Wellies are great for splashing in puddles. The soles are **watertight** and keep you dry.

➡ These thin leather soles also stop the ballerina **slipping**.

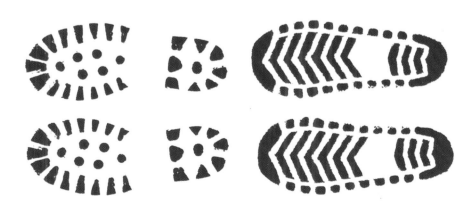

Clothes from around the world

A sarong comes from Malaysia. It is made from one piece of cloth and can be wrapped around the body in different ways.

Hard-wearing denim jeans were made for American gold diggers over a hundred years ago.

Now they are worn every day by lots and lots of people!

➡ **Native Americans first made moccasins from animal skins.**

Can you see how these slippers are similar to moccasins?

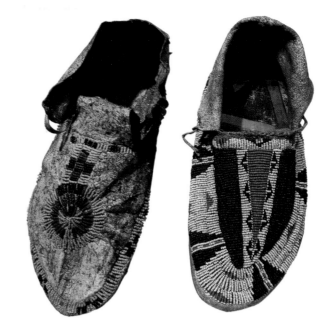

eye opener

This Panama hat is used in sunny weather. Real Panama hats are made from palm leaves. They can be rolled up tightly.

Amazing Designs

Look how **imaginative** the designers have been with their ideas for these clothes!

➡ This fish-shaped watch would be **fun** to wear.

⬇ How **warm** do you think this unusual hat would be?

⬆ Do you think you could **run** for the bus in these shoes?

These trousers are so **enormous** that you and a friend could fit in the legs! But when they are worn by an adult, they fit just right.

Think about the **design** of the clothes you wear every day. Can you think of some new designs?

Index